Emma Thomson's

felicity Wishes®

Perfect Ponies

and other stories

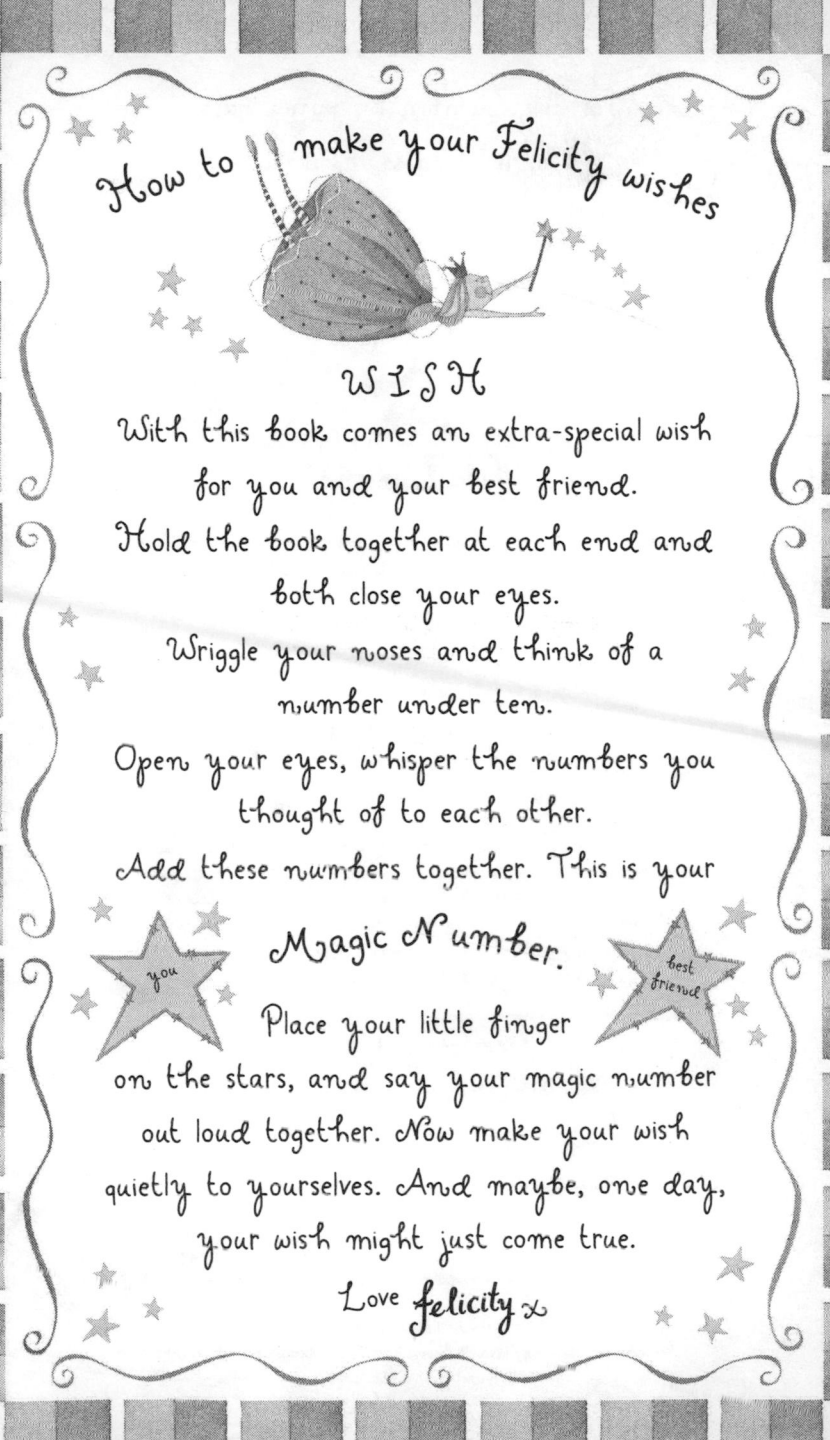

How to make your Felicity wishes

WISH

With this book comes an extra-special wish
for you and your best friend.

Hold the book together at each end and
both close your eyes.

Wriggle your noses and think of a
number under ten.

Open your eyes, whisper the numbers you
thought of to each other.

Add these numbers together. This is your

Magic Number.

you *best friend*

Place your little finger
on the stars, and say your magic number
out loud together. Now make your wish
quietly to yourselves. And maybe, one day,
your wish might just come true.

Love *felicity* x

For Jill Zambinski, pony guru
with thanks, Emma

FELICITY WISHES
Felicity Wishes © 2000 Emma Thomson
Licensed by White Lion Publishing

Text and Illustrations © 2007 Emma Thomson

First published in Great Britain in 2007 by Hodder Children's Books

The right of Emma Thomson to be identified as the author and illustrator of this work has
been asserted by her in accordance with the Copyright, Designs and Patents Act 1988.

I

A Catalogue record for this book is available from the British Library.

ISBN: 978 0 340 94394 6

Printed in the UK by CPI Bookmarque, Croydon, CR0 4TD

The paper and board used in this paperback by Hodder Children's Books are natural recyclable
products made from wood grown in sustainable forests. The manufacturing processes
conform to the environmental regulations of the country of origin.

Hodder Children's Books
A division of Hachette Children's Books, 338 Euston Road, London NW1 3BH
An Hachette Livre UK Company

CONTENTS

Circus Cheer

The Fairy Circus had come to Little Blossoming! Felicity Wishes, Holly, Polly, Daisy and Winnie had spent most of their Saturday morning queuing for tickets they weren't sure they were ever going to get.

"I'll give up being a fairy if we don't get in!" said Holly dramatically as she looked longingly at the circus poster.

"The acrobats look such daredevils!" gushed Winnie, staring intently at their costumes.

"It's the clowns I want to see!" giggled Polly.

"I can't wait to watch the perform- ing ponies," said Daisy, stroking their image on the poster.

Felicity raised her eyes to the sky and shook her head. "Oh, Daisy! Ponies are silly! They're not even magical!"

"These ones are!" said Daisy. "They can fly!"

Felicity exchanged knowing looks with Winnie, Holly and Polly. All fairies knew that ponies couldn't fly. The circus ponies were made to look like they could fly with strong harnesses and invisible wires. But none of them wanted to spoil the illusion for their unwitting friend.

"Yes," said Felicity earnestly to Daisy. "I'm sure circus ponies can fly!"

And as she looked up, Felicity saw that the queue had moved on and they were only ten fairies from the front.

* * *

At last the big night arrived. Each of the friends had deliberated for days as to what they were going to wear. The circus was performed in a large and airy big top that was bound to be cold. But Felicity knew that the heat of the excitement generated from so many flapping fairy wings could make it very warm indeed.

Felicity had finally settled on a neat short-sleeved dress, layered with a cardigan and jacket. But even before she had sat down she had removed her jacket. As she took her seat she laid it carefully across her lap.

Acrobats quickly descended from the peak of the big top in a swirling, twirling mist of sparkledust. They leapt and balanced, flew and flipped across the circus ring in ways the fairies had never seen before.

"Look up there!" hissed Holly under her breath as she pointed to the far side of the tent where she could just make out a glittering, wobbling shape hovering above the crowd's heads.

"What is it?" Daisy whispered back.

"It must be part of the performance," said Felicity quietly. "It's getting bigger."

"It looks like one of the acrobats," squinted Holly. "She's on the tightrope!"

And within seconds, all eyes were fixed, not on the acrobats performing a pyramid in the middle of the ring, but on the single acrobat wobbling hesitantly along the mile-high tightrope... without wings!

Gasps of suspense filled the air as fairies watched unblinking, their hands squeezed tightly together.

"She's going to fall!" cried Felicity, distressed.

"She's wobbling all over the place and there's not even a safety net to catch her!" Polly gasped.

The performing pyramid fairies had stopped what they were doing now and they too were watching fearfully. Slowly and carefully, but without much skill, the tightrope-walking fairy was putting one foot in front of another on a rope that was not much wider than the ribbon in Felicity's hair. Several times she misplaced her footing and was able to balance herself just in time. But as she reached the middle of the rope she stopped dead.

"She's lost her nerve," said Holly, terrified. "She can't go on!"

"Someone will have to go up there and save her," said Polly.

"But just think what that will do to her career and her confidence for ever!"

cried Felicity. And, without a second thought, she shouted out as loud as she could, "YOU CAN DO IT! GO ON! YOU CAN DO IT!"

And suddenly every fairy in the circus top was clapping and chanting, "YOU CAN DO IT!" too.

Slowly and dramatically, the fairy on the tightrope lifted one foot gingerly up into the air to place it in front of her. The audience fell immediately silent, not wanting to distract her. As she brought it down she misjudged its place, and, in what seemed like slow motion, the fairy began to wobble one way and then the other, more and more.

The audience could hardly believe what they were seeing and some had stood up, ready to leap into the air to catch her.

And then suddenly the fairy on the tightrope fell! Felicity and her friends were frozen with fear. They wanted to do something, but found all they could do was stare, mouths open wide, unable to believe what they were seeing.

In a flash, the whole big top was filled with a bright white light! And from nowhere a beautiful, strong and dazzling pony flew with speed so swift it created a breeze.

Within seconds of the fairy falling, the pony had caught her to land on his back. As he brought her carefully down to the ground, the crowd went wild!

Everyone had stood up and was cheering!

The pony, in acknowledgement,
raised himself up on his hind
legs and brayed to the audience.
The fallen fairy was safely
smiling in wonder and
waving with glee.

* * *

After the show, Felicity and her friends still couldn't quite believe what they had seen.

"I told you ponies were the best!" said Daisy.

"You're right," admitted Felicity. "They're not silly at all. I felt sure that pony was looking right at me. He was very clever, and amazingly talented."

"Did you see how the pony's friends gathered round him at the end, as if to congratulate him?" asked Polly.

"I know!" said Felicity. "I hadn't realized until then that ponies had feelings."

"Oh, they're just like us," said Daisy. "They feel things in exactly the same way as we do."

"I'm going to see if I can get a photo of the star pony on my phone," said Felicity, reaching into her jacket pocket.

"Oh!" she said suddenly. "My phone's not here! It must have fallen out in all the excitement."

"We'll wait here for you if you want to go back," said Polly kindly. "Look," she pointed, "the big top's still lit up."

So Felicity flew as fast as she could back to the big top. It looked so much bigger when empty. Quickly, Felicity found where she had been sitting and got down on her hands and knees to feel about the ground.

"Everyone's gone," said a gruff fairy voice. "I think it's safe to talk."

"That went very well," said a squeakier voice. "I think the audience really believed I was just about to fall."

"Yes," agreed the gruff voice, "good acting on your part and a fantastic, faultless performance from Star."

Felicity froze. Oh, no! The perform-ance was a fix!

"Terrible shame that we're going to

have to leave Star and his team behind," said the gruff fairy.

"Are you certain about that?" questioned the squeaky fairy. "You haven't found a way that we can transport them for the Circus World Tour with us?"

"If only ponies could fly!" said the gruff voice.

"You know, Star and his friends are going to be very upset. The circus is their life and they won't have much without it," said the squeaky voice.

Felicity sneaked a quick look at the two fairies so that she could recognize them if she saw them again. She had heard enough. Grabbing her phone, she fluttered out of the tent and back to her friends before she was caught. And what a story she had to tell.

＊ ＊ ＊

The next day was a Saturday. Felicity had planned to go shopping, but now she had something much more important to do.

She sent a text to her friends: "Going 2 circus 2 take photo of Star. B there in 30 mins. C u there. Fx".

All the circus performers had set up camp in the far corner of the field where the big top dominated. Star and his friends were lazily eating grass in the sunshine when Felicity, Holly, Polly, Daisy and Winnie approached.

"Hello!" called out Holly as she climbed up on the fence.

Star continued chewing, which was clearly more important to him than socializing with fairies. Felicity lifted up her camera.

"Hello!" she called out.

Immediately Star stopped chewing, raised his head and seemed to smile right at Felicity.

"I'm not going to get a good picture from here," she moaned.

"You're not thinking of getting in the field with them?" said Polly, panicking.

"Just to take a photo of Star," said Felicity, "and then I'll come straight out."

She lifted up her leg and swung it over the top of the fence. But as she did so she lost her balance and suddenly she found herself, skirt and tights ripped, hanging upside down.

Polly hadn't even had time to berate her friend about her irresponsible actions before Felicity had suddenly been unhooked, flipped, flung into the air and found herself riding high on Star's back! Felicity screamed, and the circus performance fairies came out to see what all the noise was about.

"He just saved me!" Felicity squealed. The circus fairies were all giggling.

"He must like you! He wouldn't do that for just anyone," said a fairy with a squeaky voice. Felicity knew it immediately as the voice of the fairy she had heard the night before.

"I had a feeling he recognized me from the performance last night," said Felicity, feeling silly. There had been hundreds of fairies in the audience.

"Yes," said the squeaky-voiced fairy slowly. "I recognize you too. I'm Molly. Can I offer you all a cup of tea? I have something I would like to ask you, privately." And she winked, raised her eyebrows and gave Felicity a funny look.

Reluctantly, Felicity jumped down from Star, gave him a big thank-you hug, and followed the circus fairy into her caravan.

As Felicity squished up on the sofa in between Polly and Winnie, the caravan door swung open and in walked the gruff fairy from the night before.

Felicity gulped and nudged her friends.

As the fairy pulled the door closed, she bolted it and turned to look at the fairies, their wings quivering in fear.

"Pleased to meet you," said the fairy in a surprisingly squeakier voice than even Molly!

Felicity looked puzzled.

"I'm Violet. You'll have to excuse me, but I'm full of a cold and I'm only just getting my voice back properly today," the fairy squeaked.

The fairies breathed a sigh of relief.

"I'm sorry to have appeared so strange and secretive out there," said Molly. "But I don't like to say too much in front of the ponies."

"Do you think they understand?" asked Polly.

"Oh, I know they understand," said Molly. "There's not really much difference between a fairy and a pony. They have hearts as good as ours, they just can't make wishes."

"Or fly," said Polly, who knew the circus's secret.

"Or speak," said Holly, beginning to think Molly was mad.

Molly and Violet said nothing for a moment, as Molly pulled a dusty book off her shelf.

"The circus is going on a world tour tomorrow. Star and his friends are going to be left behind and as we see it there are only two options: either we find new homes for the ponies, or they learn how to fly so they can come with us."

Holly nearly swallowed her biscuit whole. "Ponies can't fly. We know it was a trick in the big top when we came to see the show."

Molly and Violet looked at each other and the whole room fell silent.

"How did you find out the truth?" Molly asked, her cheeks bright red.

"I accidentally overheard you talking after the show last night," said Felicity, frowning. "You can't leave the ponies behind! Animals are for life!"

"We know, that's why we wanted to speak with you," Molly said, opening the first page of the book. "We were told this book holds the ancient instructions for how to teach a pony to fly and talk. It takes a dedicated fairy with a natural bond with the pony to make it work. We've been trying to teach them ourselves for years and we've had a small amount of progress but, I'm afraid, we've run out of time. The Circus World Tour calls."

"Why are you telling us all this?" asked Felicity.

"Because you, Felicity, have a natural

affinity with Star. It's highly unusual. I saw it in Star's eyes last night at the show. He singled you out almost immediately."

"I thought I was imagining it!" said Felicity. "I know he definitely recognized me when I called out to say hello today."

"He didn't only recognize you, he saved you from a horrid fall. Star wouldn't do that with just anyone. There is something special between the two of you and I believe that you could teach Star to fly. Then he could teach his friends."

"But you leave tomorrow! Surely that's not enough time," said Felicity.

"Take all the time it needs," offered Violet. "Star may never learn to fly, and he may never rejoin the circus, but if you don't try then we'll never know."

Felicity was suddenly overwhelmed with happiness. She realized that this was her chance really to do something good. If ponies could fly, let alone speak, it would change the lives of fairies everywhere. Then she had a thought.

"How many friends does Star have?" she asked.

"Four," answered Violet.

"I don't have room to keep five ponies," said Felicity doubtfully.

"You won't have to," offered Holly. "Five ponies is one pony each! We'll help you, Felicity!"

Felicity nearly pinged off her seat with excitement. "Really?" she said, turning to each of them.

"Yes!" said Daisy, who had already decided that the white one called Orchid would be hers. "And I'm sure Fairy Godmother would let us use her stables."

"Definitely," said Holly, who had singled out the one with the long dark mane called Storm.

"One hundred per cent," said Polly, who had chosen the neat brown pony called Magic as hers.

"Only if I can look after the wild one called Sea Wind," said Winnie.

"Then it's settled," said Molly. "I was

afraid that tomorrow was going to be a day filled with sad tears. But now I know they're going to be happy ones!"

And, rushing out to join their new pony friends, Felicity, Holly, Polly, Daisy and Winnie knew that a brand-new adventure was just about to begin.

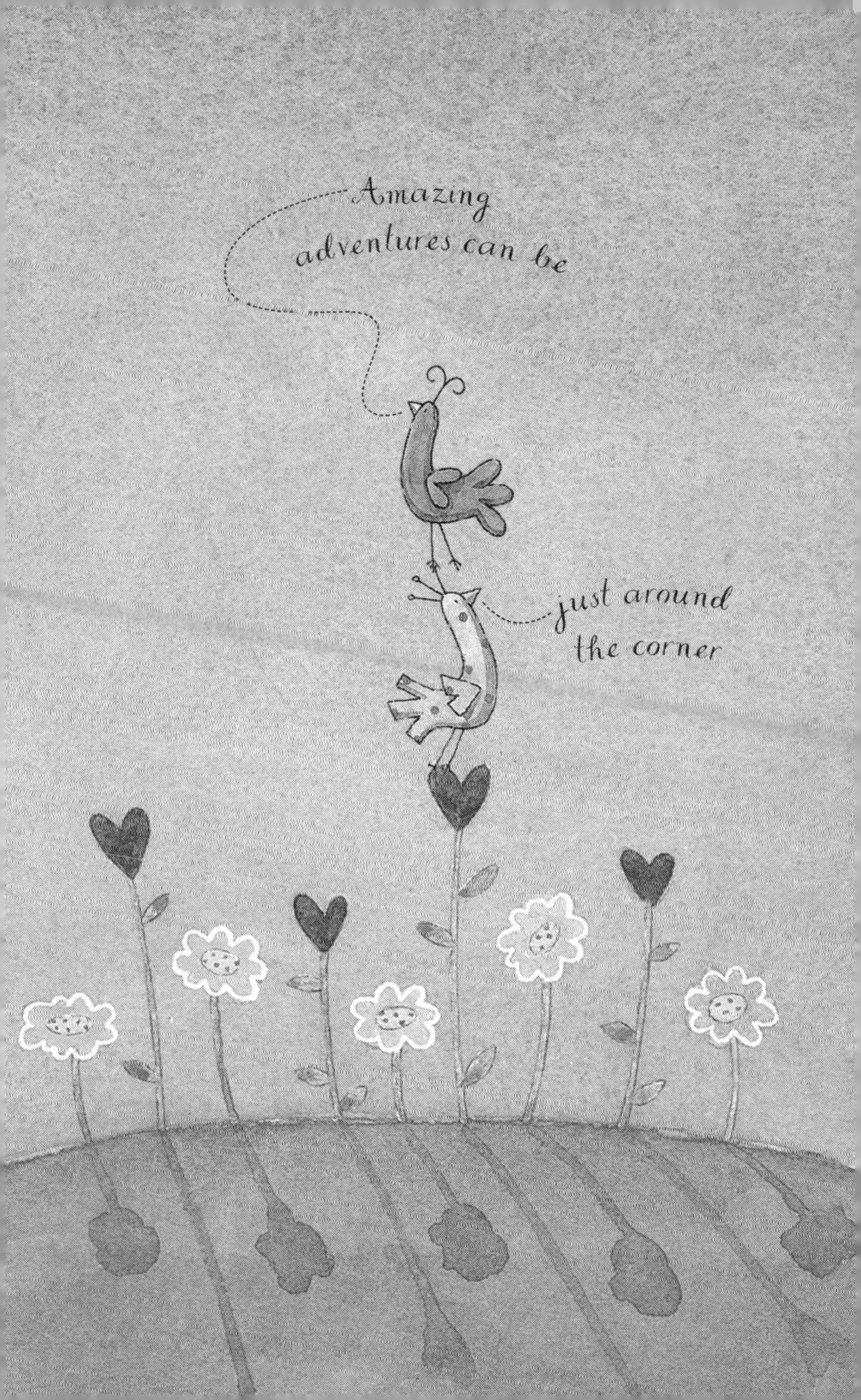
Amazing adventures can be
just around the corner

Perfect Ponies

Felicity Wishes had got used to getting up early. There had been a time in her life, when she first started at the School of Nine Wishes, that she could lie in until half past eight and still get to school on time (sometimes!).

But Felicity's lie-ins had ended the day she had said 'yes' to adopting a pony called Star. Star was worth every hour of sleep she missed in bed and more. Together with his four friends, Star had been a circus pony. Unable to fly across the ocean, Star, Orchid,

Storm, Magic and Sea Wind had been left to say goodbye to their performing friends as they embarked on a Circus World Tour without them. Luckily, Felicity, Winnie, Holly, Polly and Daisy had been more than happy to give them all new homes.

"I'm here, Star!" Felicity called out as she landed by the field gate. But Star didn't need calling; he was already waiting for her. All the circus ponies had exceptionally good hearing. Felicity didn't know it, but the second she took to the air, Star could hear the flap of her wings coming towards his field.

As usual, Felicity pulled out a carrot from her right-hand pocket and in her familiar way she began to shower Star with attention and compliments.

"Goodness, you're looking handsome this morning," she told him, giggling and patting him affectionately on the neck. "Your mane's shining golden in the sunshine and your eyes are twinkling blue!"

Star leant towards her affectionately.

"Now," began Felicity earnestly, taking a step back to show Star she was talking to him seriously. "I'm going to be a little late when I come to ride you after school this afternoon."

Star looked attentively back at her with his ears straight up, eager to understand what she was saying.

"I've got to go to the wand mender's. Polly will be here to ride Orchid, though, and I'm sure she'll come over to say hello to you too."

After contenting herself that Star was happy, healthy, safe, and had enough water to drink during the day, Felicity reluctantly waved goodbye to her new best friend.

* * *

Felicity already had a fairy best friend, Polly. She had known Polly for as long as she could remember. But the friendship that Felicity shared with Star was something different entirely. She trusted him with everything, even the secrets she didn't want to tell Polly.

Polly, Holly and Daisy were also enjoying their new-found friendships with their ponies. Daisy hacked round the woods with Orchid every evening, searching for new species of flowers.

Polly couldn't bear to be parted from Magic so took him for long rides every morning and evening. And Holly spent every spare moment combing Storm's mane, decorating his hair with ribbons and buying him the latest pony accessories.

But not all the fairy friends that had adopted circus ponies were having the same experience.

Winnie wanted to be an adventure fairy one day. She had chosen her pony Sea Wind because of his wild and untamed mane. When she saw him, she imagined the two of them leaping into exciting adventures together. But Sea Wind's mane was messy for only one reason that Winnie could see. He was too reluctant to have it brushed! In fact, Sea Wind was reluctant to do pretty much anything, except eat grass, sleep and enjoy the warm feeling of the sun on his back.

Snore

For overenthusiastic Winnie, having a lazy pony was proving a bit of a problem. And at break-time that day at school it was all she could talk about.

"He doesn't want to do anything!" she burst out, exasperated. "He's so boring that I have to admit, when there are so many more interesting thing to do, seeing him doesn't come top of the list."

Daisy put a comforting arm around her friend's shoulder. "There must be a reason behind it. I'm sure he wasn't like this at the circus."

"I've got to pop to the wand mender's straight after lessons," said Felicity, "but I'm happy to meet you afterwards at the stables to see if Star and I can help."

"Thanks, Felicity. I just don't know what to do," said Winnie.

✳ ✳ ✳

Even though Felicity had told Star she was going to be late, she could tell that he was a little anxious at not seeing her. Felicity had never owned a pony before Star and hadn't realized how important it was to be consistent with their routine.

As usual, he was waiting for her, and after giving him his carrot Felicity told him all about her day and Sea Wind's problem. Once she'd saddled him up, Felicity and Star set off to meet Winnie in the next field.

When they got to Sea Wind's field,
Winnie wasn't anywhere to be seen.
It was a full hour before Felicity heard
the familiar flap of fairy wings.

"Oh, oh!" burst out Winnie
breathlessly. "Sorry about that. I left
straight after school, but as I was flying
over Cloud Nine I saw they had just
built a new climbing wall. And, you
know me, never one to pass up an
adventure…" Winnie stopped short
when she saw the unusually stern face
that Felicity was pulling.

"What?" said Winnie checking her hair. "Sorry I'm a mess, but I was flying at top speed."

Felicity shook her head.

"Not my hair? Oh!" said Winnie, with a sigh of relief. "Your cardi! Sorry, you left it on your coat peg at school and I didn't think you'd mind if I borrowed it."

But Felicity said nothing and shook her head solemnly in disapproval again.

"Not my messy hair, not your cardigan?" said Winnie, exasperated. "Then what?"

Felicity slowly turned her gaze towards Sea Wind's field.

"Ah!" said Winnie with a sharp intake of breath. "Where's my pony gone?"

"You didn't even notice, did you?" said Felicity. "Star and Sea Wind are enjoying themselves playing together in the next field. There's still plenty of daylight. Why don't we go for a ride together?"

Winnie blushed. "Because of how Sea Wind's been recently – you know, with no enthusiasm to do anything – I haven't really been riding him. I haven't polished his saddle, brushed his coat or oiled his hooves for ages…"

"Never mind about that," urged Felicity. "We can have a pony makeover after our ride!"

Sea Wind was reluctant to let Winnie saddle him up and get on his back, and if it hadn't been for Star's encouragement Felicity suspected that he might not have walked with Winnie on his back at all.

✳ ✳ ✳

Felicity had learnt a lot about the surrounding countryside recently. It was a place she'd only flown over before to get to Sparkle Beach or have the odd picnic. But now she knew all

its intricate bridleways and pathways.
Lacy summer shadows fell on the
fairies' backs as they rode slowly along
the country lanes until they came to a
grassy field.

"Let's try a canter!" said Felicity,
letting Winnie go ahead.

Winnie sat deep in the saddle,
touched her legs to Sea Wind's sides

and raced off, hooves thudding on the grass.

When they stopped both fairies had wide happy smiles on their faces.

"That was incredible!" said Winnie.

"Great, wasn't it!" said Felicity.

"I didn't think anything was as much fun as having an adventure, but that almost was!"

"Then I've got an idea," said Felicity, who had been thinking a lot about Sea Wind and Winnie as she rode. "I don't think Sea Wind is a lazy pony. I know he doesn't have much enthusiasm, but with a little bit of magic I think we can change that... together."

"How?" asked Winnie.

"I think it might help if Sea Wind and Star share a field together for a while. And perhaps we could visit our ponies together and go for a ride like this every afternoon."

Winnie was eager to agree.

✴ ✴ ✴

The pony makeover
Winnie and Felicity
had given their
ponies after
their ride had
been so much
fun. Sea
Wind had
surprised
Winnie by
allowing
her to brush
his coat until it shone like silver.

All ponies love to be given attention
and made to feel special.

But to Felicity's disappointment it
had all been in vain.

After they had brought Sea Wind
over to Star's field, Winnie promised
to meet Felicity the next day at 8 a.m.
sharp, before they flew to school. But
at 8.30 Winnie was still nowhere to be
seen.

"Oh, Sea Wind," said Felicity. "I'm lucky Star doesn't get jealous. Without Winnie here there's only me left to tell you what a beautiful pony you are. You look amazing after your makeover."

Sea Wind whinnied gratefully, but Felicity could see in his eyes that she was no replacement for Winnie.

When Felicity finally caught up with Winnie at break-time she could barely get a word in edgeways, Winnie was so busy talking about her morning.

"Thank goodness, you're OK," Felicity finally got to say. "So, another adventure was more important than seeing your pony?"

Winnie looked awkward. "No!" she protested. "I knew you'd be there and Sea Wind was OK, wasn't he?"

Felicity frowned.

"I'm sorry, Felicity. Let's go for a ride after school instead," said Winnie apologetically.

Felicity flew off and sat under the Large Oak Tree to think. She was sure there must be a way to help Winnie and Sea Wind bond. She took out her mobile phone and called Molly from the circus; maybe she knew something about Sea Wind that could help.

✳ ✳ ✳

"I've decided to take you somewhere different to yesterday," said Felicity to Winnie as she saddled up Star next to Sea Wind that afternoon.

"Oh," said Winnie disappointedly. "I was looking forward to another canter."

"This will be much more fun, I think. It's a place I've never been to before, but I've been told it's very exciting," said Felicity, feeling a little guilty about her first white lie.

"Let's go then!" said Winnie as she mounted Sea Wind and followed Felicity out of the field.

The sunny windy track the ponies

began walking down gradually got
more and more difficult to manoeuvre.
Overhanging branches arched across
from either side to make what seemed
at times like a leafy
green tunnel.

"Are you
sure this is
the right way?"
asked Winnie.
She pushed
another branch
out of the way
before it hit her
in the face.

"Erm… yes…
I think so," said Felicity, faking her
uncertainty. "Look, there's the forest
over there!"

And ahead of them Winnie could just
make out a dense, dark jungle of trees.

"We're going in there? On a sunny
day like this?" she said in disbelief.

"Yes," said Felicity happily. "In the middle, there's supposed to be a beautiful clearing with a track that takes you up to the top of a hill – and you can see the whole of Little Blossoming."

Winnie loved an adventure, but she and Sea Wind followed uncertainly. It didn't look like there would be any clearing in the middle of such dense wood. And, if she had been honest, usually fearless Winnie would have admitted to feeling a little bit scared.

"It's so dark," she whispered. "How do you know where we're supposed to be going?"

"I don't," said Felicity, telling her biggest white lie yet. "I have no real idea how to get to the clearing. I was hoping that we'd just sort of find it."

Winnie winced. Forests and woods were enchanted places, but they often held their dangers too.

"What was that?"
squealed Winnie as
she heard an eerie
noise ahead
of them.
"Oh!" said
Felicity,
pretending to
be scared too at
the noise she had just
made herself.

"I don't like this," admitted Winnie
finally. "Let's find this clearing, and
quick!"

It was just the cue Felicity had been
waiting for.

"Why don't we split up?" she
suggested. "We'll have double the
chance of finding it that way. And
whoever finds it first leaves their pony
and flies to find the other."

Not thinking straight, Winnie agreed.
"You go that way, and I'll go this

way," urged Felicity. "See you soon – I hope!"

* * *

Knowing the way all along, Felicity found her way to the beautiful clearing easily. Within a matter of minutes she had secured Star's reins to a nearby tree and taken to the air.

It wasn't long before she saw Winnie not far from the point at which she had left her. Just as Felicity had planned, Winnie was heading towards a steep rough bank covered with sharp brambles. Felicity remembered clearly how Sea Wind's delicate footwork had earned him extra applause at the circus. And she hoped with all her might, as she hovered, that Sea Wind would remember his old skills.

"Oh, no!" she heard Winnie cry out when she saw the steep bramble hill. "We're stuck. We'll never get down here. Sea Wind, STOP! Don't go forward…"

Suddenly full of doubt that she was doing the right thing, Felicity found it hard to watch.

But she needn't have worried. Sea Wind was doing better than picking out the bramble-free patches with his hooves. He almost appeared to be dancing! And what's more he looked as though he was enjoying it… and so was Winnie, who was actually laughing!

But as soon as they got through the brambles, Winnie's smile faded. Ahead of them the ground appeared to fall away into an enormous gushing water-fall.

"Even the award-winning Water Fairies couldn't cross this without drowning!" Winnie cried to Sea Wind. "Felicity, we're stuck! Where are you? Felicity!" she called out in vain.

Felicity had to fight with her conscience not to give herself away as she hovered quietly above them, obscured by the trees leaves.

Winnie began to sob and hugged Sea Wind's neck for comfort. Had it not been for her secret, Felicity would have flown to Winnie's assistance immediately.

Sea Wind had been given that name for a reason. As a young pony, he had lived by the sea and had learnt to swim from an early age. Before long, he had developed the capacity to swim so fast that his speed took him up and out of the water. From a distance it appeared as though he was gliding gracefully over the surface.

Felicity's wings were aching and just as she tried to adjust her straps she heard a horrible scream.

"NOOOOOOOOooooooo," shouted Winnie. "HEEEEEEEELLLLLLP… We're… Oh, my goodness, we're… running on water!"

And Felicity looked down to see Winnie riding high in the saddle as Sea Wind showed her what he could do best.

When they got to the other side, Felicity had landed and was waiting for them.

"That was amazing!" gasped Winnie.

"Follow me!" Felicity said, and she led Sea Wind and Winnie through to the clearing.

"I'll race you to the top!" Felicity shouted, not giving Winnie a moment for recovery.

And within minutes the two ponies were galloping up the hill side by side. With the wind in their hair and their hands on the reins, both the fairies felt bound to their ponies. Their movements were fluid and Felicity and Winnie felt like they were flying!

When they reached the top of the hill, Winnie couldn't speak for ages. She just lay against Sea Wind's neck. And when she did finally speak, it wasn't to Felicity, it was to her pony.

"Thank you," she said as she jumped off to come round to his side. "I'm afraid I may have been neglecting you and our potential and I won't ever do it again. That was the best adventure I've ever had."

"You make a great team!" said Felicity and hugged them both.

As Felicity walked Star back to the stables, she noticed that the most beautiful, rainbow-coloured stripe had appeared on his tail. "This is the start of something truly magical," she whispered into his ear.

It's always fun
doing new things

with friends by your side

Flying Fantasy

Felicity Wishes and her friends Holly, Polly, Daisy, and Winnie had each adopted a pony. The circus they had once belonged to had embarked on a tour that had taken it to the other side of Fairy World. Because the ponies couldn't fly, they had been left behind.

The circus fairies had also left behind a huge, dusty, leather-bound book that held the only key to reuniting the ponies with their circus family.

"You don't seriously believe all that

stuff?" scoffed Holly as she peered over Daisy's shoulder at the book's yellowing pages.

"The instructions for teaching a pony to fly sound so simple," said Daisy, pondering the drawings.

"If it was simple there would be as many ponies in the sky as there are birds!" said Polly, giggling at the thought.

Felicity shuffled up next to Daisy and took hold of one side of the heavy book. "I've tried it time and time again," she said, tracing her finger over the eight easy steps. "But everything goes wrong when you sprinkle the sparkle-dust at stage four."

"That's as far as their old circus trainer got, wasn't it?" asked Winnie.

"Hmmm," said Felicity, "and she'd been trying to teach them for years!"

"Maybe," mused Polly logically, "this book is just fiction. None of us have ever seen a pony that can really fly.

There's no one to say it really works."

Felicity, despite how much she wanted to believe, had the same doubts as Polly. The book looked authentic enough, but there were chapters that seemed even more incredible than the one they had all be focusing on.

"I think we should throw the book away and start again ourselves, in our own way," ventured Polly.

"I think we should just stop trying altogether," said Holly.

"Maybe you're both right," said Felicity, who was thinking of the ponies. "I've been going through the same four steps with my pony, Star, every evening after school for over three weeks now. It's definitely time for a break."

So all the fairy friends agreed for the time being to give up trying to teach their ponies to fly. Polly ceremoniously folded shut the enormous pages of the book and dropped it in the recycling bin. And, with it, she ended the dreams their ponies had of rejoining the circus.

* * *

Fairy life went on much in the same way as it had before. The friends attended the School of Nine Wishes during the day, and when the bell sounded for the end of the last lesson Felicity, Holly, Polly, Winnie and Daisy flew as fast as they could to the stables where their ponies waited for them.

Most nights they each saddled up and rode together over the hills that

surrounded Little Blossoming. But at
weekends, when they had more time,
they spent hours grooming their
ponies' coats, combing and plaiting
their tails and oiling their hooves
until they shone.

The fairies
and ponies all
seemed to be happy,
but Felicity had started to
worry. On two occasions she
had caught her pony Star leaning
out over his fence – not yearning for
the grass on the other side, but looking
towards the hills and the sea. When it

happened a third time Felicity knew she wasn't imagining it. And even though Star couldn't talk, she knew he was missing his friends in the circus and longed to join them.

That night, Felicity had a dream that she was racing Star. Star's hooves were thundering so quickly they hardly touched the ground and then, in an instant, they really had taken to the air and were flying high above the clouds, leaving the race far below them. When Felicity woke up and found herself hovering above her bed, holding her pillow, she knew what she had to do.

* * *

"I'm going to start trying to teach Star to fly again," said Felicity to her friends at school the next day. "I know it's impossible and that we've all tried our best already, but I have to – for Star's sake."

"I saw you scribbling something in

your book during chemistry," said Polly, "and it didn't look like the experiment you should have been copying down."

"You're right, it wasn't," said Felicity, excitedly rummaging around in her bag, "It was this…"

Felicity opened her chemistry book and turned the pages round to face her friends.

"Wow!" said Holly excitedly, turning it up the other way. "What is it?"

"I had a dream!" said Felicity, not answering her friend directly. "When I woke up I suddenly had an idea. What was the first thing we did before we learnt to fly?"

Daisy thought back to days she could barely remember as a wingless fairy.

"We practised waving our arms," she called out.

"Before that," hinted Felicity.

"We jumped off low walls," said Holly.

"Even before that… come on… you must remember," she said, glancing round at her friends' blank faces.

"It's a day none of you will ever forget!" Felicity urged, giving them a hint by turning round, wiggling her bottom and flapping her wings.

"We bought draught-proof knickers?" guessed Holly.

"We bought our very first pair of wings!" said Felicity incredulously. "These are the plans for how I am going to make Star his first pair of wings."

"But the big leather instruction book didn't say anything about pony wings," said Polly.

"And we all agreed that the book's instructions didn't work," said Felicity. "I'm certain these wings will!" She closed the book, pushed it back into her bag and took to the sky. "See you on Monday!" she called out, leaving her stunned fairy friends behind her.

* * *

Star was bemused. First Felicity had been tickling him with a tape measure all morning, and now she was sneezing and giggling under a mountain of feathers.

When she finally emerged she was holding the most enormous bird Star had ever seen. It frightened him but as he took a distressed step back, Felicity peeped her head over the top of the wings.

"It's me, silly!" she said to Star.

"These," she said grandly, "are going to help you fly!"

Star whinnied in a confused sort of way.

"Now, stand still and keep your head up," Felicity instructed him. Then she heaved the wings above her head and then let them gently down on to Star's shoulders.

After a bit of adjustment and securing, Felicity stood back. "Perfect!"

she squealed, clapping her hands and bouncing up and down in the air. "Now you really look like a pony that can fly!"

Instead of going through the same four steps she had been teaching Star from the old book, Felicity used her own method. She would like to have thought that it had come as the result of years of scientific research, but really Felicity was making it up as she went along.

"OK," she said uncertainly as she took out a tempting carrot from her pocket. "Come and stand up here."

Star looked at the carrot, and then at Felicity, who was standing precariously on top of a wide low wall in front of him. He didn't want to disappoint his new fairy friend, but being in the circus had taught him all about safety issues.

"Come on," urged Felicity. "Look, it's

easy!" she said, showing him as she jumped down to the ground. "Use your wings to balance you."

Star laid his ears out to the sides. Gingerly, he lifted his front two hooves on to the wall.

"Good boy!" encouraged Felicity, letting him take a bit of the carrot. "Now your back two."

Star stayed put. He could feel the wall wobble beneath him.

"If you do this, then we'll be one step closer to finding your friends across the ocean," tempted Felicity.

Eager to please and against his better judgement, Star transferred all his weight on to his front legs, and lifted up his back ones to jump on to the wall as well. With the helpful shove Felicity gave him from behind, Star was finally standing awkwardly on top of the low wall. Felicity gave him the rest of the carrot.

"Now," said
Felicity, holding
out her arms
as if to catch
Star, "use
your wings
to balance
and...
JUMP!"

Busy
munching his
carrot, Star felt
his balance shift... and instead of
jumping he felt himself tumble in slow
motion towards Felicity.

Felicity was frozen. She didn't know
whether to save herself and jump out
of the way, or stay where she was and
cushion Star's fall.

In the end it was a mixture of both.
As Star landed awkwardly on the
ground Felicity found herself pinned
to the floor by her wings.

"Oh, oh, oh!" was all Felicity could say above Star's painful whinny.

Wriggling frantically, she freed herself, and was immediately at Star's side.

"Oh, Star!" called out Felicity. "Are you OK?"

But by the whinny that continued to leave Star's mouth and the deep heavy breaths he was taking in through his nostrils, he obviously wasn't OK.

"Oh, no!" she cried out, seeing the

cut on his leg. "You're hurt, I've hurt you! Oh, how dreadful. Stay right where you are. I'll go and get help."

Felicity called Polly to come and look after Star whilst she flew as fast as her wings would carry her to the Vet Fairy's house.

The vet was called Miranda. And despite being in the middle of her lunch Miranda packed up her bag of equipment and came immediately with Felicity to where Star was still lying.

Gently moaning now, Star looked the unhappiest Felicity had ever seen him.

"It's all my fault," said Felicity, explaining the feathered wings that still stuck out from under her pony. "I was trying to teach him to fly."

Miranda had seen all sorts of animal disasters, but she had never seen anything like this! She set to work straight away and within minutes she had cleaned the wound, given Star something to ease the pain and was scanning his leg with her laser wand.

Polly put a gentle arm around her best friend. "It'll be OK," she said, trying to sound optimistic.

"Oh, if only ponies could speak," sighed Miranda. "The scans are inconclusive. I really need to know whether this is a superficial sprain or whether the ankle is broken. I daren't risk helping him on to his feet if he's broken his ankle, but if it's just hurt he'd be fine to get up."

"So he's OK lying down either way?" asked Polly.

"For the time being," said Miranda, looking at her watch. "But it won't be long before it's dark. It will be chilly this evening. If he stays here overnight we risk him catching a cold, which is the last thing he needs."

Felicity buried her head into Star's mane and began to cry. "Oh, I'm sorry,

I'm sorry, I'm sorry!" she said again and again.

Polly held Felicity's hand tight. No words could make Felicity feel better, but at least she knew that Polly was by her side.

"Now, now," said Miranda firmly. "Star is stable and he isn't in pain. The best thing you two can do is stop crying and fetch blankets to keep him warm. I've got another appointment to go to now, but I'll come back as soon as I've finished and we'll see if there's been any improvement."

Back at Felicity's house, she and Polly didn't only get blankets, they picked up some water and a large bag of carrots. As Felicity grabbed her mobile phone out of her bag, she also pulled out the failed flying instructions she'd dreamt up in chemistry.

"Rubbish," she said resolutely as she opened her recycling bin to throw them away. And as she did so, she saw the brown leather book open on the page that read "Teach your pony to speak".

"Anything's worth a go, don't you think?" she said to Polly.

"I really think we should wait for the vet to…" Polly trailed off. Felicity was already out of the door and flying off to rejoin Star.

The sun was already setting by the time Felicity and Polly got back to Star. He was grateful for the water and carrots. After covering him with a blanket and snuggling down next to him Felicity picked up the large brown book, propped it on her lap and opened it.

None of the fairy friends had bothered reading the long introduction before. The wordy section with no pictures had seemed boring and a waste of time. But now, Felicity focused hard on every word. Anything was worth a try.

* * *

The superior-grade sparkledust, collected from the ancient and endangered multi-star flower from Petal Mountain, must be used when performing this magic. No alternatives can replace it. You will find a small envelope on page 84 that contains a sample for your convenience.

* * *

Felicity had barely been able to get the final words out and narrowly missed stepping on Star's foot as she jumped up to shake the book open at page 84. A small golden envelope fluttered to the ground.

"Oh, my goodness," exclaimed Polly. "No wonder the instructions didn't work before. We had the wrong sparkledust all along!"

"I can't believe it. Star is really going

to be able to speak… and maybe even fly!" said Felicity, trying to keep calm.

Slowly and carefully, with a smile beaming across her face, Felicity opened the envelope. "It's empty!" she said, looking inside and letting out a long disappointed sigh.

But Polly sensibly tipped the packet upside down and shook it over

Felicity's hand. Several tiny diamond-like sprinkles tumbled out and landed in her palm.

"I spoke too soon!" Felicity said, suddenly aware of the enormous preciousness that she was holding in her hand. "And soon Star might speak too!"

Felicity and Polly followed the book's instructions to the letter. And when Star spoke, it was with a voice so soft the fairies weren't sure if they'd imagined it.

Felicity leant close to Star's mouth to hear his words. In a gentle whisper, he told her he thought his foot was fine to move, that he did not blame her for his accident and that when he was rested he was looking forward to flying!

When Miranda flew back to join Felicity and Polly, Star was already on his feet. At first she was very cross, but she soon saw that he was much better – thanks to Felicity.

"There was no way of knowing his ankle wasn't broken. What you did, getting him to stand up like that, was an enormous risk," Miranda reprimanded.

Felicity looked down at her toes.

She had to keep Star's ability to talk a secret, at least until there was enough special sparkledust from Petal Mountain to be available to all the ponies in Fairy World.

"I'm sorry," she said. "It seems as though I've had a lot to be sorry for today."

"And a lot to be grateful for too," said Miranda. "You're very lucky it's just a sprained ankle and that you have a wonderfully brave pony. When his foot is mended I'm sure he'll take you on lots of amazing adventures."

"I know," said Felicity, looking up at Star and giving him a wink. "Adventures I've only dreamt of until now!"

If you really
believe in magic

it can come true!

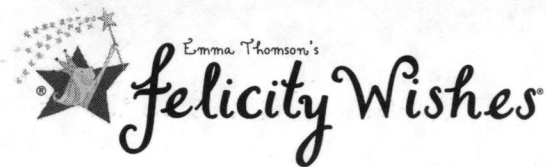

Felicity discovers

the hidden mysteries

of a bookshop in

Storytelling Stars

Book Bamboozle

Felicity Wishes was in her English class at school – but she wasn't paying attention!

"Felicity, what topic have you chosen?" asked Miss Page.

Felicity looked up sheepishly at the teacher.

"I haven't chosen one. I don't know what to do," she replied quietly. "I looked in the library like you said, but I couldn't find anything."

Miss Page had set the class individual projects, writing about subjects of their choice. It was easy for Holly, Polly, Daisy and Winnie. Holly loved anything to do with fashion and had decided to write about the development of fashion through the ages. Polly wanted to find out more about being a tooth fairy. Daisy chose to write about plants and flowers and their natural habitats and Winnie was doing her project on the great fairy adventurers of the past. They had all tried to help Felicity, but none of them could think of a topic that interested her.

"Don't worry, come and see me after class, Felicity," Miss Page said kindly, with a reassuring smile.

"We'll see you by the Large Oak Tree," Polly called when the lesson was over. She fluttered out of the classroom and into the warm sunshine outside, while Felicity stayed behind.

"Right then, Felicity," Miss Page

began. "Can't you think of anything to write your project on?"

Felicity shook her head.

"And you couldn't find anything in the library?" Miss Page continued.

"No, nothing," Felicity replied.

"Well, there's one other place you could try."

Just then there was a knock at the door and Miss Fossil, the history teacher, fluttered in. She swooped up to Miss Page's desk, put down a note and quickly turned to fly back out of the classroom – without uttering a single word. Meanwhile Miss Page continued to talk to Felicity, without any sign that she'd seen Miss Fossil.

"As I was saying, have you ever been to Little Blossoming Bookshop?" Miss Page asked.

Felicity shook her head. She'd never even heard of it.

"It has old and new books on every

topic imaginable. It's always worth a try if there's nothing in the library," Miss Page told her. Then she drew Felicity a map of where to go and Felicity left to join her friends.

✳ ✳ ✳

"It was very strange! She didn't say a word," said Felicity, now sitting under the Large Oak Tree.

She had just told Holly, Polly, Winnie and Daisy about Miss Fossil coming in to see Miss Page and neither fairy speaking to the other.

"Actually, I'm not sure I've ever seen them talking," said Polly thoughtfully.

For the rest of the day the fairies carefully watched Miss Fossil and Miss Pen. They sat at opposite ends of the teachers' table in the cafeteria at lunchtime, they didn't look at each other when they passed in the corridor, they were never both in the staffroom at the same time, and they left the school by different doors at the end of the day.

"It's very odd," said Daisy as the fairies fluttered home. "The other teachers talk to each other all the time. I wonder what they fell out about."

Read the rest of

Emma Thomson's

Felicity Wishes

Storytelling Stars

as Felicity turns detective

and reunites the teachers.

If you enjoyed this book, why not try another of these fantastic story collections?

Designer Drama

Star Surprise

Clutter Clean-out

Newspaper Nerves

Enchanted Escape

Whispering Wishes

7 Sensational Secrets

8 Friends Forever

9 Happy Hobbies

10 Party Pickle

11 Wand Wishes

12 Dancing Dreams

13 Spooky Sleepover

14 Fashion Fiasco

15 Pink Paradise

16 Spectacular Skies

17 Dreamy Daisy

18 Perfect Polly

19 Winnie's Wonderland

20 Holly's Hideaway

21 Fairy Fun

22 Starlight Songs

23 Crowning Cure

24 Fairy Fame

felicity Wishes

Storytelling Stars
and other stories

Storytelling Stars

felicity Wishes

Perfect Ponies
and other stories

Perfect Ponies

felicity Wishes

Glittering Giveaways
and other stories

Glittering Giveaways

Look out for these five special editions

Summer Sunshine   Holiday Hullabaloo

felicity Wishes

felicity Wishes

felicity Wishes

Christmas Calamity

Winter Wishes
and other stories

Snowy Showdown

Christmas Calamity   Winter Wishes   Snowy Showdown

SEE YOUR FRIENDSHIP LETTER HERE!

Write in and tell us all about your best friend, and you could see your letter published in one of the Felicity Wishes books.

Please send in your letter, including your name and age, with a stamped self-addressed envelope to:

Felicity Wishes Friendship Competition

Hodder Children's Books, 338 Euston Road, London NW1 3BH

Australian readers should write to...
Hachette Children's Books
Level 17/207 Kent Street, Sydney, NSW 2000, Australia

New Zealand readers should write to...
Hachette Children's Books
PO Box 100-749 North Shore Mail Centre, Auckland, New Zealand

Closing date is 31st December 2007

ALL ENTRIES MUST BE SIGNED BY A PARENT OR GUARDIAN.
TO BE ELIGIBLE ENTRANTS MUST BE UNDER 13 YEARS.

For full terms and conditions visit www.felicitywishes.net/terms

Friends of Felicity

Carley Cresswell is my Best Friend because you can tell her your bestest Secreats and she wont tell any one. She is like a Sister to me. We do everything together we have been best freinds Since we were Seven. If im upset she always cheers me up we will be freinds forever nobody can split us apart. Carley is also my Bestest freind because she never lies we do what best friends do she is the funniest and bestest person in my life I am doing this for Carley to show how much I like her.

Georgia Golightly
age 9